STECK-VAUGHN

PAIR-IT BOOKS™

Horse Feathers!

Written by Manuel Hoyo

STECK-VAUGHN
ELEMENTARY · SECONDARY · ADULT · LIBRARY

A Harcourt Classroom Education Company

www.steck-vaughn.com

Some horses are huge and strong.

Some horses are small and light.

Some horses run to win races.

Some horses run to herd cattle.

Some horses have socks.

Some horses wear shoes.

 7

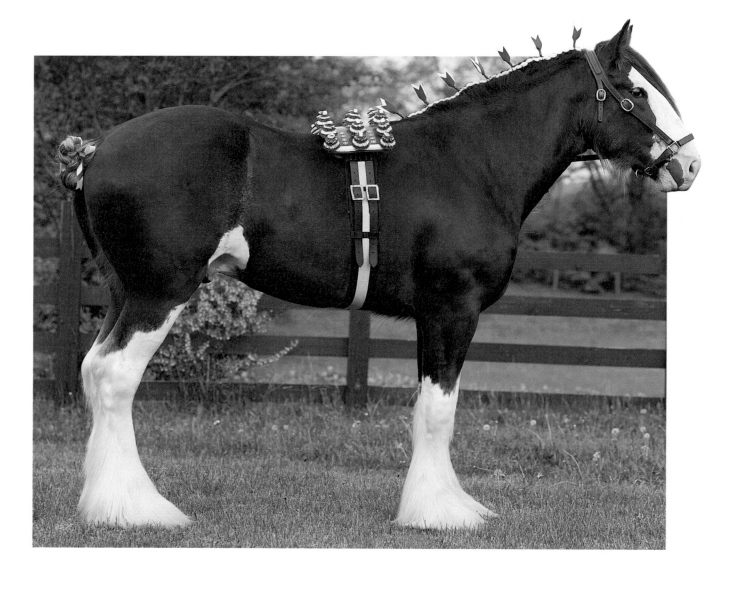

Some horses have feathers on their legs.
Horse feathers!